SNOW

Uri Shulevitz

SCHOLASTIC INC.

New York Toronto London Auckland Sydney
Mexico City New Delhi Hong Kong

ISBN 0-439-13144-8

12 11 10 9 8 7 6 5 4 3 2 1   9/9 0 1 2 3 4/0

Printed in the U.S.A.   49

First Scholastic printing, September 1999

For
Margaret Ferguson

and for
Kiddo

The skies are gray.
The rooftops are gray.
The whole city is gray.

Then

one snowflake.

"It's snowing,"
said boy with dog.

"It's only a snowflake,"
said grandfather with beard.

Then
two snowflakes.
"It's snowing,"
said boy with dog.

"It's nothing,"
said man with hat.

Then
three snowflakes.
"It's snowing," said boy with dog.

"It'll melt," said woman with umbrella.

A few snowflakes float down
and melt.

But as soon as one snowflake melts
another takes its place.

"No snow," said radio.

"No snow,"
said television.

But snowflakes don't listen to radio,

snowflakes don't
watch television.

All snowflakes know
is snow, snow, and snow.

Snowflakes keep coming and coming and coming,

circling and swirling,
spinning and twirling,

dancing, playing,
there, and there,

floating, floating through the air,

falling, falling everywhere.

And rooftops grow lighter,
and lighter.

"It's snowing," said boy with dog.

The rooftops are white.

The whole city is white.

"Snow," said the boy.